Treasured Tales

Little Red Riding Hood

p

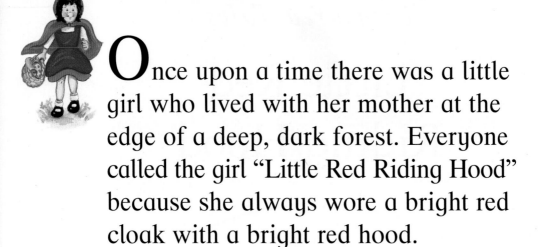

Once upon a time there was a little girl who lived with her mother at the edge of a deep, dark forest. Everyone called the girl "Little Red Riding Hood" because she always wore a bright red cloak with a bright red hood.

One sunny morning her mother said, "Granny isn't feeling very well. Will you please take this basket of goodies to her, to make her feel better?"

"I will," replied Little Red Riding Hood.

"Remember," said her mother, "stay on the path, and don't stop to talk to any strangers on the way."

Little Red Riding Hood hopped and skipped along the path to Granny's house. She had only gone a short way into the deep, dark forest, when a sly, nasty wolf with big shiny teeth and long sharp claws jumped out onto the path, right in front of her.

"Hello, my pretty one," said the wolf. "Where are you going on this fine morning?"

"Good morning," said Little Red Riding Hood politely. "I'm going to see my granny, who isn't feeling very well. She lives all the way on the other side of the forest. But please excuse me—I am not allowed to talk to strangers."

"Of course little girl," sneered the crafty wolf. "You must be in a hurry. Why not take a moment to pick a big bunch of these lovely wildflowers to cheer your granny up?"

"Thank you Mr. Wolf. That sounds like a very good idea," said Little Red Riding Hood, putting her basket down on the ground. "I'm sure that Granny would love them."

So, while Little Red Riding Hood picked a bunch of sweet-smelling flowers, the wicked wolf raced ahead through the deep, dark forest and soon arrived at Granny's cozy cottage.

The wolf lifted the knocker and banged hard at the door.

Granny sat up with a start. "Who is it?" she called.

"It's me, Little Red Riding Hood," replied the wolf in a soft voice just like Little Red Riding Hood's.

"Hello, my dear," called Granny. "The door is not locked—lift up the latch and come in."

So the wolf opened the door and, quick as a flash, he gobbled Granny up. Then he put on her nightgown and nightcap, and crawled under the covers to lie in wait for Little Red Riding Hood.

A short time later, Little Red Riding Hood arrived at the cottage and knocked on Granny's door.

"Who is it?" called the wolf, in a high voice just like Granny's.

"It's me, Granny," came the reply, "Little Red Riding Hood."

"Hello, my dear," called the wolf. "The door is not locked—lift up the latch and come in."

So Little Red Riding Hood lifted the latch, opened the door, and went into Granny's cottage.

Little Red Riding Hood couldn't believe her eyes. "Oh, Granny," she said, "it is so nice to see you, but what big ears you have!"

"All the better to hear you with," said the wolf. "Come closer, my dear."

Little Red Riding Hood took a step closer to the bed.

"Oh, Granny," she said, "what big eyes you have!"

"All the better to see you with," said the wolf. "Come closer, my dear."

So Little Red Riding Hood took another step closer. Now she was right beside Granny's bed.

"Oh, Granny!" she cried. "What big teeth you have!

"All the better to eat you with, my dear!" snarled the wolf, and he jumped up and swallowed Little Red Riding Hood in one BIG gulp!

Now it just so happened that a woodcutter was passing Granny's cottage that day—he was on his way to work on the other side of the forest. He knew that Granny had not been feeling very well, so he decided to look in on her.

What a surprise he had when he saw the hairy wolf fast asleep in Granny's bed!

When the woodcutter saw the wolf's big, fat tummy, he knew just what had happened.

Quick as a flash, he took out his sharp, shiny ax and sliced the wolf open! Out popped Granny and Little Red Riding Hood, surprised and shaken, but safe and well.

The woodcutter dragged the wolf outside and threw him down a deep, dark well so he would never trouble anyone ever again. Then he, Granny, and Little Red Riding Hood sat down and ate all the lovely, yummy goodies that were in Little Red Riding Hood's basket.

A little while later, Little Red Riding Hood waved goodbye to her Granny and the woodcutter and ran all the way home to her mother. And she didn't stray once from the path or talk to *any* strangers!